PICKING THROUGH THE STONES

10. Mai '92

Liebes Ehepaar
Reimann

Ein kleiner
maltesischer
Zeitvertreib

Mit den besten
Wünschen
Ihre

Anita Laster

D1727116

PICKING
THROUGH
THE
STONES

Notions, Nostalgia and Nonsense

Poems

NICHOLAS DE PIRO

SAID INTERNATIONAL LTD.

SAID INTERNATIONAL LTD.

Published by:
SAID INTERNATIONAL LTD.
43, Zachary Street,
Valletta - Malta

First published 1991

Printers:
Printwell Ltd. - Malta

ISBN 1 87 1684 55 2

Copyright © 1991 Nicholas de Piro

CONTENTS

PRESENTATION

My day of reckoning is every day,
I may have slept on straw or asphodel last night,
Was gone away outside the threat of life,
Today I faced the truth again,
Was introduced to me, told it was I,
The saint, thief, first of men,
Some god or bankrupt, behind bars,
A fugitive,
The father of forsaken mouths,
The butcher of the camps,
The mother of the Pope,
The husband of the Queen,
An oracle, poet,
Failure's son,
Dying, aged and diseased,
A youth, lover, warm and craving,
Hungry, satiated, pickled, salted, plastered,
Wise, black, foreign,

Every day the introduction comes,
And every night is lost to innocence,
And if I dream, or do not dream at all,
I still awake surprised, relieved or saddened
By the introduction.

Much of life is poetry:
History, ambience, who knows?
Landscape, Oriental charm,
Occidental wit, Botticelli's calm;
The great Arabian nose - no nose,
Negro lips, - some lips
Are poetry;
The bosom of Ambrosia,
Her navel,
The Chateau of Lafitte,
And cheese from mountain goats;
Memories, so many thoughts,
And childhood,
Music I remember,
Perfect novels,
Discussion with old friends,
Little victories;
Starting points.
The confidence of youth,
Squalor's brightest laughter;
Wise eyes of receding health;
The angst of great adieus;
Not truth nor ever death,
But often faith,
Where breathes good poetry,
And love
Is faith as well.

MR JAMES GOING UP

The steep old staircase climbs away
As dawn is shafting spangles
Onto piano photographs
All out-of date.
My little plum-tree fills the bowl with mature fruit,
An Adam's apple plays along my boy's new stubble.
A youthful tittied friend sits on the piano-stool,
'Good morning Mr James did you sleep well last night?'
What lovliness! How sweet those buttered lips!
Where have I scaled dark hidden steps
And promptly reached this fifth?
The bellied justice full of saws!
Am I to wear a laurel crown,
Tell everyone to heed my new-found state?
'Have you retired Mr James?'
'No I have not.'

ON MY OWN IN THE RAILWAY CARRIAGE

How fast the noise
and twilight
through all windows
fixed for wide;
I look, alone,
speeding, driven
by nobody I can see
who is employed by British Rail
on this wide evening.

A slant to left
a lurch to right
vague rushing forms
make way
for me to pass
the distance towards
this journey's end,
and still
my soul is breathing grassy air
and I am I.
Am I delivered,
from all here?

I wish
this feel
of beat and beat of breath
to blow forever,
languish,
in the never ending
record searing
heaven scented
hurtling
lasting now.

BONES

What do I care about your bones
Or mine or anybody's bones;
Your eyes, if they should glance again
Your hands grip mine,
I would not think about your bones.

I will remember you as once
I held you eager on the sands,
When time was ripe and love came fast
And lingered on, remained alive;
And memories too -
But bones are bones.

PRETENSION

Let me confess I orgied with Porphyria,
not so to boast I am more able, rich
and utterly virilious,
so blessed - see my works,
I give each day and look afar
my own ambition pacing,
nor do I tread without consideration.

Now kiss me wheresoever here! take charity
my masted, moored and moulded Aphrodite,
so be for me forever and modulate dear opposite,
come modulate for me Melinda.

A muse is come so that I scratch new thoughts,
poeticalities around those trained to live
by others far away and gone,
some long, long, long ago,
whose swelling chests became extinct.

Possessions do not cry to be surrendered
lovingly or not. They live on carts
which we must ride,
so I shall sing rose-lilily to you Melinda,
for I live, perhaps tomorrow still,
until I heave away my bones pre-packed
to rest along a way.

A private day I want,
a faithful thing to say,
and pray for yet another day,
more waiting times to play,
and if you need to understand
loan, give this singing heart another beat,
or come, lock up behind your heavy day,
and see that wild pretensions sing
on flags and marble plaques,
and think of life somewhere.

ON MORTALITY

I feel I want to live on Earth
When I hear things that move my wits
To fantasise and hunger on,
And these are mainly music, song
And some dear voices.

I thought of one old friend today,
How she believed in endless art,
How we could never speak again
And have our usual interchange,
For now the grasses grow
And lie between the two of us.

I saw the written slabs above
The heads of people I have known,
I spoke to one how long ago,
Whose stone was being put in place?

I read the books that claim to know,
And they are clear on one point
That it will happen soon or late,
And then they differ, more or less,
And others more, so much sometimes,
That there is breadth wherein to choose
A hundred paths, to run into an open space,
To hide, to guess, to solve, try to believe
A meaning for this mortal state,
The pain for which no palliative,
Nor antidote exists except blind faith.

I live, and everyday I hope for one more day,
And fear and sorrow tell me all they know
Of friends I do not see,
But I can watch a little,
Then unwilling move away and on
Behind the power to survive all time
Enchanted by the force that parts.

ONE NIGHT OF THE PAGAN GOD

Camomile grew wild that summer,
Placid monks were singing Terce,
Waiting, books all read,
For him to call a willing face,
Move on and go elsewhere.

The band was dumb at four a.m.,
The players gone to bed, asleep,
With flesh quite bare and conquests made,
And he could call a sleeping face,
Move on and go elsewhere.

He passed within the urban light,
Crossing flag-stones on his toes,
He shrieked alone in granaries,
And then again from ranges' peaks,
He shone, but for himself alone.

He saw a loving fond princess,
He saw a man who looked unwell,
There was a dog, a cat, a cow,
He smelt the scents and noxious smells,
Of life, which he had made himself.

He did not sleep that usual night,
He did not sleep, not ever yet,
He could not die for he was one,
Who managed death and could not fade,
Or lie, or ever be in debt.

He could not share with finity
He could not make himself more gods
He could not be except himself
He could not jest with his own strength
He could not take but make and give an end.

The band was dumb at four a.m.,
Placid monks were singing Terce,
Waiting, books all read.
The players gone to bed, asleep,
With flesh quite bare and conquests made.

And camomile grew wild.

I danced in my straits with the lame girl I loved,
I held her so close to my heart that she cried,
The rain made us happy that lame girl and me,
And we laughed till we fell, then she sighed a deep sigh,
And smiled as she said we were free as the free,
And no, no one could set us apart.

The moon bore us witness that indigo night,
As we parted with colour and mime,
I climbed every branch with my burden of love,
And our wounds held us fast as so often they'd done,
Then I carried her limp to the stars far above,
And descended into the light.

CANCER CO.

My name is life
yours forgotten
gone each year each week each day
you bear the fruit
I am the happy chance that stays
to eat and drink
you bear the fruit of life
and die
I live.

More people live
on it
to buy
and pay
their way
than slop
their life
in it.

A LITTLE LADY

There was a little lady who died on Friday night,
I know she'll be forgotten very soon,
She was a gentle little spinster who lived a tidy little life,
And they buried her on Monday afternoon.

She'd knitted for the missions when she'd had the time to spare,
But was busy with her hospital round too,
On a Monday and a Friday, she'd not missed a visit yet,
And her smile was slight and subtle but came through.

Her heart bore just one sorrow from so very long ago,
Her man had died for England on the Somme,
I don't remember hearing very much about his deeds,
But I think she may have said his name was Tom.

FATAL CLICHES

Aspiration ends where lethargy begins,
with hope and effort spent -
it ends. At last
the grand surrender comes,
despair sleeps,
and thrust of vision dies,
and victory is gone elsewhere.

Listen,
I shall speak the truth,
but how, or where,
except for those who know.
Who knows?

The no of logic is
so mortal, yet
the earth reflects
rebirth
for someone's sake,
the new leaf or the memory.

Rain and sun, youth, beauty,
drought, disease, mirages of sorrow,
fear and lonliness, scorn, envy,
good and tiring work and greed,
giving, begging, coming, going,
questions, answers, knowing, loving,
longing for, smiling at, waiting with
the deep-set eyes of wisdom,
hoping beyond the rank is colour,
thinking like, believing in, the great
who now have gone to eat and drink elsewhere
for someone's sake,
and death ploughed in will nourish,
as before,
the harvest's plenty.

IN TRANSIT

What matter here in this calm place,
To feel a hand upon the shade,
And integrated ask this day,
Between the sense of angled heights,
Or contours of some patient walls,
If balm like this might hold the lids
And shutters of a compact peace
Besieging light's deceitful ray;
Where still papyrus holds green courts
Upon a cool triangled mind,
This curtained whim collected by
A charabanc perhaps too soon.

GRAND PASSIVE

I tasted the aura of petals
puffing 'Entendu'
all the way to the top
floor by floor
slanting
lift shafting
through to the blur
of the sky.
I slumped
falling fathoms
of mattressed history
declaring, expostulating,
swimming, loving, loving,
and I'd not eaten of the clouds
nor made an exit.
I could die a thousand times
and still want more.

Blue undetermined
elongated sloggings
through the valves
of nature's mood
condescending, overflowing,
fermentation
still replacing,
living on
re-fuelling
strong as Hell is long,
dark as cold
mould,
rhythmic
and constant.

The time was spent but life lived on,
And neighbours jubileed their dates,
The streets were spangled for a prince,
And someone died on the third floor
Just one below the studio where
An opera played through the day,
And on a theme a sight returned
Of innocence, the years gone by,
Of pain and waste and options lost.

The time was spent but life lived on,
With Father, Mother, at the house,
Broth cooking, rain, and crocuses,
And my old bed and window-sill,
And bright eyes tugging at the bell,
Dear Harriet Grey and yes, old George,
White clouds, the grass, the leaves, the night,
Tall curtains and the highland fling,
And voices still not gone away.

The time was spent but life lived on,
And love was practised by the poor,
And art was made and locked in vaults,
The earth fermented and dislodged,
And wells were filled, the trees performed,
And skies declared the great unknown
To witless prancing parasites,
And paths were taken for a stroll,
And an inventor washed his hands.

HARMONY

A cemetery should be seen from the air;
It is not a sombre entirety;
Its lugubrious mouldings are lost,
And appear as natural as furrows in a ploughed field
Or the indented shadowings of corn crops
That fit easily, belong,
Like the city river's arches
Or the prisms of a street.

It is gone,
And the sunset is splendid tonight.

APPLE

I swam among the cowslips
And sat in clear seas,
I entered virgin forests
And climbed to beacons' peaks,
While hilltops looked around all green
And sang so airily,

I drank the water of the spring.

But times are changing faster
And needs and musts are thick,
And India's mouth is gaping,
China, Africa are waiting,
Brazil, half the world
Are furnaces of want,
Puffing clouds of need so new
That ultra rays of violet
Violate the sun's life-shine,
To crack the ways
A god of love composed
For perfect balance.

I drank the water of the spring.

But times are changing faster
I did not know the wants and craves
Of Science turned to puberty,
I had not heard the cries,
The laughs, the Evine lust,
The hunger knowledge could excite,
Till Academe, arcahic, spoke
Supporting moral sense
And sensitivity,
To stem the quickening of minds
That wage the ultimate from scholarship
At any cost.

I drank the water of the spring.

But times are changing faster
And Science has tasted sin.

THE DOUBT OF GREENE AND PHILBY

Scattered, together they wonder,
Wanderers looking away,
There is no more discussion between them,
There is nothing that is left to say.

Ardent, emphatic and loyal,
A Roman, a Marxist and bound,
By faith they have kindled and fostered,
By answers each claims he has found.

There is doubt that must not be admitted,
There is sadness that comes from the doubt,
There is bitter frustration and closeness,
As both need to hold hands and shout.

Closer together than brothers,
Faithful without unity,
They have suffered alone and together
For the spirit that sets all men free.

INTERVENTION

Why create
and give away a will?
Would not clockwork do?

Is there something in your nature
not like logic: art perhaps
or even whim and jest?

The gods, do they have hearts -
play games, guess,
but never intervene?

O you
you are incorrigable
perfection -

do not interfere:
not in plague, injustice, war,
innocence crushed,

nor even death ...
Christ Jesus did
alone.

He took the agony of man:
'Why have you forsaken me
Father?'

Father?
You made a human heart as great as you are strong,
with substance holy beyond thought,

liquid, precious, tender, flowing,
touching Mozart as he wrote the Lacrimosa,
Raphael when he painted the Transfigured,

Francis of Assisi, Mother Theresa,
The Little Flower, unfeigned martyrs,
the knowing, the saints,

the brave, the serving, the sorrowful,
the unbelieving Voltaire, Marx and Bertrand Russell,
gullible hordes. And yonder still

the seeking nations: blacks, Indians,
Mongols and millions unending,
ploughed and always waiting.

'See me,' he said, 'you see the Father.'
Our Father who art
where are you this day

to give us our daily intervention?
Consume a cruel unremitting need,
dissolve the will, the doubt,

so might this creature-son be clothed in you,
faint his heart and weary,
left to himself he cannot do for you,

keep him God-Father,
intervene, not later,
for Christ's sake.

LIFE FLASHES

Life flashes,
and is the tunnel long?

Life climbs,
and is the hill so steep?

Life gasps,
and is the heart that stout?

Life fails,
and are the arms of love
the only destination?

So help me come and help me Monday
sun hide where is a black wet cloud
Abu wake up damn you Tuesday
wake, wake, wake up,
why you keep staring
like you cannot see me?
God save us! Do you hear me Wednesday?
Somebody will come
little one do not cry
trust me, I know Thursday
sit quiet sit
oh your knees
you have fallen on your knees
do not try to walk
somebody will come
soon, very soon.
You died Friday
gave all that blood.
Where is it?
We want it now!
By your blood
make it rain
everybody cry
to Heaven Saturday
God remember milk and honey
here we are
open your arms everybody try
time is short it is yours God
see this woman's breasts
her child is still
and does not cry
I am on my way I tell you
if you don't hear soon
I shall complain in person.
Where is everybody Sunday
where is light?

PROMISES

A promise that, one day,
All of this one day;
More promises in store,
Quite soon,
Then very very soon;
Another one tomorrow,
Tomorrow in the post;
And still I listen,
To perhaps the voice of love,
Or fame. The crinkle
Of ten sacks of promise-notes,
Sworn to fall crumpled
In this lap of mine;
And I can hear
The greater promise
Of a way to view
Beyond horizons.

BLACK ROUNDEL WHITE

Blame it on the blacks and you can be sure
It is their violence, arson and attacks
That we will live with, suffer without law
Blame it on the blacks.

I've seen the Brixton mobs with gun and axe
And peace gone from our streets for evermore
And this is why our people pay a tax.

Christ's love! It is a full cup to endure
And nature rides the easy road, is lax
While tribal man bids here for even more
Blame it on the blacks.

Blame it on the whites let all men know it
Our fate is only hope, we have no rights
Tell them of our cross and how we bear it
Blame it on the whites.

I've seen the Ethiopian trecks and sites
Where death sweeps cruel, hard and definite
The homelands in the south, dark days and nights.

Christ's love! It is a red cup free to split
And when he gives it all, still there are plights
And nations take no heed of any writ
Blame it on the whites.

Blame it on the blacks
Blame it on the whites
Blame it on the blacks
Blame it on the whites
Blame it.

POEM

O Sorrow,
Wait until tomorrow,
My heart clings to peace for today.

O Pleasure,
You don't last forever,
Yet be with me now and stay.

O Life,
It is torment and strife,
That you're heir to, oh why?

O Death,
Your kiss takes my breath,
And I'm with you for aye.

THE CHAMPION

I put my strength and ardour to the test;
And passed through fearful long and narrow paths;
And thought I had attained a dire need;
To own and then proclaim an envied prize.

I dreamed a tired dream and there I saw;
In gardens where the fruit of knowledge blooms;
Myself, with claims unstaked and rendered false;
My orb now burdened in another's palm.

I thought about the loss I had sustained;
And as I 'woke my term was all too short;
For the sweet cause of longer-lasting time;
For setting out to search quixotic fame.

My heart did plead, and I did grieve;
Then wisdom came one day and told me this:
'Laugh, laugh, forever laugh!' And I did laugh;
And now I sing the joy that's my belief.

SONNET

Indeed! I thought, and then I thought again,
Of touching toes, gnats, hawkers on the street,
Of balustered verandahs and warm rain,
Of spilling drinks on hotel cotton sheets.

I tore him limb from limb, and then I cried,
'Archangel keep your sword - the fire's past'.
I watched and was alone. I nearly died,
While sighs and stabs of sorrow held me fast.

A stumble one find morning on the train,
No sparkle left in me nor any punch,
I typed my way through bouts of salty rain,
And then turned down the boss's son for lunch.

My love came back a liar and a sinner,
I bowed my head when he suggested dinner.

MRS DANCY

Dearest pumpkin
Eleanor of Aquitaine
Joan of Arc
Helen of Troy
Isabella
Boadicea
Theresa of Avila
Mrs Thatcher
Madame Recamier
Maria Theresa
Lady Godiva
Saint
Little devil
All in one
Pink cheeks
Fat bum
Keep smiling
No wonder Fred
Loves you
And your little
Cabbage patch.

Here on a pang
of yesterdays
starts the slither
down the arm
of love eternal
trespassing
pitfalls
O 'tis I
I
Sir Someone's chubby little boy
perceiving not a little rub
a-coming down
a soft and buttered age
to glide
fistful fast and bubblesome
I saw you
shooting grace
a-race with gods
by light
in time of stars
or whatforevers
for whom?
Broom!
Are we not dead?
Are we not dust?
I think
I do
ahem!
Oi be awake
O aye 'tis I
dear dear Belinda
shall we mate
and go to sleep again
and again
and again
and again
and again
and again.

ROUNDEL

I saw despair alone, her veils were dropped,
Her hand stretched out, she waited for me here
And there and here again in comfort propped,
       I saw despair.

She sang no song nor smiled nor showed a care,
She walked recantless round me, sometimes stopped
And sat to look at me from near.

But then she went away and let me opt,
For what I do not see and cannot share,
I stood, still, frail, again, on crutches, propped,
       I saw despair.

RHYME

You are lovely Veneranda,
Rouser of confusing candour,
In my soul excitement, panic,
In my heart fixation, manic,
On my knees a worship cringes,
On your touch this reason hinges,

Soporific Veneranda,
On your breath let me meander,
Deep into my being wander,
Veneranda! Linger languor.

EXPERIENCE

Having drunk some tiresome cup
and thinking it was deep, unique
in fact, experience to contribute;
and whether it was the deep at all
or not, one bores.
With ageing hunger to prove usefulness
one tries, enhances yawns, the fate
of certainty bestowed.
When furnaces of life
abate and new thoughts feature
but are mostly lost,
make way for others'
lesser thoughts perhaps,
there lies hidden deep a pain
to numb the lust one needs
to climb the hills,
but love survives,
somehow,
and still one wants to live
and share.

JUNK

Three pictures on the floor
'Mrs Barlow's clearance.
There's tables too, some chairs,
oak, a dresser, more in store.
And I'm not 'anging 'em in my 'ouse.'
I pondered on the forms,
and mused on, just a little,
lost in focus, searching through
a thumping agitation.
No signature; no clue,
'Yes, I would like to buy them.
No, Doris you must not,
you cannot give them please.
What do you mean
you'll throw them out,
they are not crude or lewd.'
The're good enough for me to take
like three most cherished relics
bundled in blankets, home.
I played a little Bruckner
before I looked again;
I drank a glass of wine,
they were, oh yes they were
much, much better.
They could be at the Guggenheim,
the Getty, the Tate.
Here is Coleridge on high,
Van Dongen at his Dongingest.
I'll keep, frame, hang
all three here
for me; oh what a find.
Now come on, bring on the experts,
'Tell me who this master is?
No simple mortal here.
You do not know? How can that be?
You're sorry,
sorry you do not Sir?'

What writer writes that when she's read,
A germination in the head
Becomes a symphony of thought
That binds forever images together?
Would it be vague go ask oneself
Of recent authors one has read
Which in a living cycle's scene
Say Belloc, Waugh or Graham Greene
burst as fresh perhaps and blest
As Vita Sackville-West?

ANSWERS

O how podgy
Are those who argue phenomenology
And will, in vain,
In terminology
That is obscure, explain.

O how lean are all the others,
Brothers who must sup
Incomprehensible solutions
And settle meanly
For perhaps a synthesis of Thomism,
When they would rather stretch to reach
For temptation on a beach.

Philosophy is bottomless.

I have spent your money bank,
On oysters at Bentley's;
Sitting at the bar with learned councel
Giving me butterflies;
His appetite.
He said,
"M'mm,
The crab: Black velvet: a tankard;
(two tankards)
Serve you a one-four-six? What to follow?
Nothing!
Did you know? Nothing ...
Nothing at all! ... Worthless:
Paper! Quite; quite, null -
i-fied.
A case?
Armagnac.
In
  - va -
      lid!
          Un
                - a -
                    ware?
Carry on as usual ... oh
Dear me."

Hindsight lives on
insulting high moralities
and harnessed notions
even atheists'
profundity shut in
to make good cant.
Truth is for believers
convicted by sweet thought
nativitating core and thud
need and lovespit. Why
heart of mine beat still
and make the world die
once for me today
and let me save old Charlie
from the bats in his Tiepolo.
Fortitude, Justice,
trumpeting Triumph Herald
buttocks face-a-face
look not too far below
at Envy's eyes well lidded
young and open hinterland
soft bosom great and wide
heaving ready for a head to hide
its aspirations deep within.
Come to me and groan
you sad and sterile mass
that I more loving than the beast
in faith shall plant a force
within your hearts
that never shall relent -
come pseuds and seedless
sodden pits of living pain
come genderless protagonists
on board
come banks of envy
hate safes of the spirit
bearers of a broken soul
Come all come all.

The future is forever and for me,
Another image of a hidden him
Whose face can hardly be researched
But causes what never had been thought;
He will not turn away,
He said one day what never had been thought
Say Father
Nor did he turn away,
Made room
In his house to fill hearts
With what never had been thought,
Sick sad sorry goaled torn lost evicted
Discarded discredited and me;
I need your anger release help strength
Councel wisdom
What never had been thought:
Tell me Father, hold me, pay the debt
So as I beg, like you I too forgive
What never had been thought.

My mind wanders
calling on that constant pain of exile
to desist,
to dream a little only,
not again today,
tomorrow.
To pretend,
oh to pretend to be at home again,
remember from afar
the playing fields of England,
log fires,
copper kettles,
thatches,
stately homes,
windy leafy lanes,
conkers on the ground, trodden on
by grassy mud-packed wellies
happily.
Rust and spleandour too,
freshly drizzled,
making blazes for a grand finale.

Then Spring is back one day,
tranquil Cotswolds,
angel-children
batting on the green,
and delicious Summer pudding,
grass and lovliness.

Once I,
in heavy scented Summers
addressed the Church of England Men's Society,
judged exhibitions,
cut ribbon.

And while I muse nostalgic now
on Gas Board ladies,
Protection of Rural England,
The N.S.P.C.C.,
with my woman in the chair,
Schubertiads for Steiner schools,
Old Devonians for tea,
salesmen from Colt Cars,
Round Table pseuds,
visitors -
hand shakes,
I wonder.

There are
Instant smiles,
Texans for the night -
'highlight of our trip Baron' -
The Smith College luncheon -
'so elegant - so gracious' -
cucumber sandwiches, o dear,
and 'What is this Buck's Fizz?'
'Oh ... no lips that touch the vine
will ever touch mine ha!'
admiration,
catering,
performing.
'Do you go back to Malta Sir?'

Yes, yes I go forever,
that I may smell the orange blossom scent,
and put my hand against a warm soft limestone wall,
and walk barefoot on čangatura floors,

splash the dark blue ocean once again,
complain about the heat,
the Mistral, lack of hygiene,
smile and be content,
among my very own,
as once before I was
and did not know it.

Example,
And fashion, architecture,
Kings, armour,
Confidence, fanfares
Orchestras, bankers
And colour

Some cheer tradition
the past and the old
are enshrined
and the aura serves well.

Cajolery,
Inveigles a course,
Winning time, inspiration,
And smiles,
Stroking temperate hearts
To heat,
The quaint, methodical
To want

All glory for honour
and laurels behold
the loved of the gods
and the aura serves well.

Then pressure
Subpoenas the gun,
Propaganda,
The threat
Kidnaps the will,
Drugs,
Re-directs reason,
Weakens,
Lets blood

Discipline wins
and discipline moulds
the moderate swear with the bold
and the aura serves well.

Bribery thrives
Both sides of a sin
And merchants,
Cede their gain,
Or gain politic thrusts
From welfare's ends;
Ideals thirst
Legends live
To stab,
While logic wanes

Excellence hums
Still all is all
Still well is well
And winners shine.

NICOLAE

I said string him up by the ankles
And his wife, hang, shoot, draw her too
And I called with the souls of the thousands
For vengance on these two

And I would have pressed any buttons
And I would have pulled a rope
And I would have whipped a standing horse
Whose cart was the only hope.

I was righteous at that moment
At that moment I was right.

Then I saw his body slumped and shot
His mighty face I could see
It looked softer, old and greying
The eyes looked straight at me

And God in Heaven it did come
It came shame and remorse
And self-disgust followed the lust
And I was sick of wanting blood
Or anybody's only breath,
Or this man's damned
Damned death.

MISSA SOLEMNIS
In Pectore Cantata

Mighty
That I may be Yours
Vivat vivat vivat.

Human fabric
Form infinite
Eternal in æternum.

Vanquish Death the Truth Kyrie eleison
Lasting Life the Dream Christe eleison
Resurrection Kyrie eleison.

Glory glory to One God glory!
Peace give Lord bestow
Caved in hearts plead of the Light
Shine accord Your rays O Bliss
More to adore
More to adore
More to adore.

Creator - sing high Seraphim
Almighty - sing low Cherubim
Ransomer! Sacrifice! - all the saints sing.

Love led Jesus to the cross
Saviour of the living throng
Love led Jesus to the cross
Saviour of the dying horde
Love led Jesus to the Cross
His to give eternity.

Blessed Spirit - Only love
Holy Son - Only way
Goodly Father - Only Father

O earthly tombs rejoice are come
The Angels with the hope of saints
The seed of Abraham is saved
Rejoice for He is come and lives
Sing ALLELUIA help me!
Sing ALLELUIA help me!
Hear me raise my voice and cry
Help ALLELUIA help me!
Hope is risen in the heart
The trumpet blares intense
O hush and let this cry appeal
O hush and let this plea ascend
Sing ALLELUIA help me
Weep my heart in gladness sing
Credo oh I do.

Invisible Holy
Transfigured O Joy
Path of all hosts
And light of the lost
Sanctifier slaughtered
Lamb of the Father
Love of the Spirit
Arisen for me
Triumphant
That I may live
Forever amen
Metamorphised
Eternal amen
Amen! Amen! Amen!
Come in His name
O Chorus of the Angels
Hosanna
Alleluia
Amen.

O GOD

Father
Your love
so great
You sent
Your son
to pay
a pen-
alty
which You
could not
withhold
from Your
very
justice
Lord must
we not
love You.

O God
redeem-
er we
pray for
Your faith
for all
of us
to see
Your gift
of love
coming
to heal
the rift
we have
crea-
ted from
absur-
dity.

PRAYER

Jesus Jesus can I ask you to relieve my aching heart,
While your hungry grope and perish everywhere,
Should my prayers help these people; O my Lord I wish to know
Are they tuly your beloved chosen for a life of woe,
Do you want my contribution, the small offer of my pain,
Are my worries of some merit, do you want them Lord again?

Jesus Jesus will you give me all the health and strength I need,
While I see the desperation of the sick,
I can hear their lamentations in a world that's full of fear,
Will you surely place them highly in your kingdom, by you, near;
Can the wretched then be blessed as you said in holy text,
Will you help me and my loved ones and all those I care for next?

Jesus Jesus I do need you to support my aims in life,
While the lonely and the homeless struggle on,
Was the plan of your creation simply just an act of love,
Will you succour them with pity when they cry to you above,
Can I then request your favour in a fulsome blinkered cry,
Will you tell me what to do dear Lord until the day I die?

ORA PRO NOBIS

Queen of the Angels
My heart is so heavy
My need is upon me
Like mountains of stone

Queen of the Angels
Believe me, believe me
And send consolation
For I am alone

Queen of the Angels
My anguish destroys me
Oh hear me, I beg you
And I shall be free

Queen of the Angels
Plead for me swiftly
And press the small hand
Of the Child on your knee.

LOURDES

(For two sets of voices - the underlined to be spoken simultaneously)

1st voices (start here)	2nd voices (start here)
	Anglais?
... priez pour nous	Francais?
pauvres pecheurs	Deutsch?
maintenant	Italiano?
et a l'heure	Oh sorry
de notre mort	Manchester
Amen Nein your under hosen!	
	Hang up your clothes over there. The towel's cold. Right
Español	on the second step we say a prayer together.
Hail Mary	Vite Monsieur.
full of grace	Attention!
the Lord is with thee	Ici ils sont des
blessed art thou among	grandes malades.
women..	

Holtz onto ze bar

Ave O Maria

piena di grazia

Il Signore e con te

tu sei benedetta fra le donne

benedetto e il frutto

Monsieur viens ici, vieni

Iz watch

Bene bene.

Thank you

God bless you

Save me
Help me.
O Mary

Nicola girasi
pray for us

Au nom du Père

et du Fils ...
Monsieur pas comme ça!
quatre personnes.

Attention!

Aaaaah!

Miserere mei

Miserere mei

Pietà di me.

Can you manage a catheter?
Oui chef, oui.

Your breast pocket?

In the name of the Father
it's alright Paddy

and of the Son
thank Our Lady

slowly feet first

Our Lady of Lourdes
...........pray for us

It's alright
St Bernadette ...

St Bernadette

                  ... pray for us

pray for us

                  Right in
                  slowly.

<u>O Mary mother of mercies
look upon this crushed
and crying creature
and gain for him ...</u>

                  change hands

steady.

                  Good - good.
                  Next one ready

Allemand
no legs

                  no legs.

O.K.

                  O.K.

No, no Spanish, Basque

                  A bishop
                  Estados Unidos

<u>Hail Mary
Full of grace</u>

                  Benedicat vos
                  omnipotens Deus

<u>Pater et Filius
et Spiritus Sanctus</u>

Lauda Sion Salvatorem
Aaaaaaah!

                  Lauda duce et
                  pastorem

<u>Dei Genetrix Ave
Ave Ave Maria Ave
Ave Ave Ave</u>

ABSENCE

Tepid fingers kiss my lips
And longing taunts my soul
To whip an ailing heart
With strokes of jealosy
And need of sweet infinity.
These heavy bones resisting still
God bless them, no! no more
God bless the scythe
That's in the winter's chill!
It will not pass me by again.
O Angelina wait,
O Angelina hear me,
I'll soon be 23
Again.

HARRY

Harry was a pragmastist. He knew.
And all along, just like a dealer
With insider knowledge,
Indulged his whims
Between soft cushions
Until the very last;
and then, exhausted
by the sport he could not face,
He left it all forgetting to say grace.

Most notable scion within the city gate
Last facric of the proud baroque,
A gilded angel blows his silver horn
To summon you to court in Elysium.

What will sustain your spirit noble lord?
You have not gleaned your myriad gifts on earth,
Nor wished to lie ensconced in ermine folds,
No great misericord your daily Jesuits' seat.
The omnibus brought solace to your heart.

O highest Alfio,
Will you refrain,
Again,
In Elysium?

ODE

Was there a vision ever formed
So calm and tall and easy;
It made one feel one's deepest core
Beyond such beauty was no more,
Love like this, who could endure?

I asked:

      "Tell me if what I see seems
Like something from the nectar dreams
Like something soothing glowing light
Like something new to a man's sight?"

I heard a voice, a song, reply
Oh I shall hear it 'till I die
And it said, "Helen."

ARTHUR BART.

There's no work for three million now;
They live in the North sea;
Where the bed produces riches,
And Arthur makes the tea.

And Arthur went to Eton first;
And then he joined the Guards;
And when he left at twenty-nine,
He'd used up all his cards.

With hardly any venture left;
He cried for a concession;
Britannia smiled on him at last,
In a small possession.

Not only does he make the tea
The oil-rig workers seek;
He makes the chips and bangers too,
For half a grand a week.

ARNOLD

He's lost his wits, he's lost his wife,
He's lost his son and daughter;
He turned on all the taps at home,
And flooded it with water.
His neighbours heard the shattering glass,
And saw the china flying;
It was all quiet after that,
And then the man was crying.

They came for him at ten past five,
That black and icy morning;
It was a van, they all wore white,
And held him, he was yawning.
He'd been to tea the day before,
And showed no irritation;
But when the Vicar's wife said, 'More?'
He spoke of masturbation.

A winsome honest thinking chap,
'I like to cogitate a bit:
And aim at worthy stewardship
And love if time permits.'
He saw the sign to Coney Hill,
And smiled and said he knew,
That all that mattered was his wife;
And love and children too.

MILKMAN

'If only I could hate her now,'
He cried and cried, 'I can't.'
She'd gone away with Harry Mogg,
Left the children and the dog,
Couldn't care a toss it seemed,
For Harry was her man,
And Graham knew it.

'She may come back again one day;
No, no of course she'll not.'
A break's a break, she wasn't free
To listen and do charity.
And though he'd worked to please her, now
It had been lost, for naught,
And Graham knew it.

While Summer shone out in her prime,
He smiled at last for one more time;
His swagger back a polished car,
He waved to all and on, not far,
He drove, he stopped in a small wood,
Exhaust, a hose and his heart stood,
It stood, it stood in that small wood,
At last,
in peace.

ARTHUR BELL

Arthur Bell you're still with us,
You laugh and smile and paint better than most,
You make new friends and plans, and full of hope
Enthuse.

He shot you in the First World War,
Some Hun, right through the head;
I wonder if he lives today and knows his deed,
Is haunted by your ghost all these long years,
Or lies remembered by a mossy cross;
But you are here, this Spring, at ninety-three,
Thank God.

FELICITA

There is no reason I should know
The manner or the way of things,
The cause, the scent, what flowers next
Why gross rewards are heaped on some,
Why merit cannot pay the bill;
Of man who lives on Cotswold hills
Or hunts in yellow on the plain
Or hunts for husks in other fields,
Or keeps a flat in Eaton Mews,
If I am safe enough to sleep
Or even rest and think away
The economic boundary;
Whose right to starve,
Whose need to die,
I do not know Felicita
A good case for propriety
Or rendering of nocturnal wants,
Why lovely evenings start in May;
What pulls me to you I don't know,
It's not the things you say.

saw the watercolour and heard rain from his study
   as he declared and qualified his ardour;
t was an oval view and just the same as I remembered
   Taranto in late September,
Church bells, and my only serenata, here to tempt me
   with a fearful crie-de-coeur;
Come to remind an old deserter of an evening and a
   dreaming of a song she must remember.

Then his Celtic fire came staccato, speaking practicalties,
   explaining prospects dull and dear;
But my heart did beat for Italy again and I felt the tender
   folly of a latin-loved princess that day again
Lest glens and mist and common sense devour my heart
   and leave me throbless with no errant whim to yearn or fear,
did now dream how Carlo tried to steer my unmolested virtue
   to desire, while his tears, song and laughter cried for me in vain.

Oh but I shall take you Arthur Ernest Thompson for my truly wedded
   everlasting upright faithful groom;
And raise your goodly little brood to come as you would wish
   the children of some Deputy Lieutenant;
And dressed in tweed and gum-boots one dim day, your old wife's span
   will reach its gothic tomb;
But she will look sometimes to see without regret, the watercolour
   on your study wall, the view of Taranto, a little pennant.

CONSTANT

My friend
Got the sack
From Jones & Hicks,
Where he was porter.

One day
The boss said,
'You're in charge of
Ladies-who-do.

Keep an eye on
Things
After hours,'
He said.

My friend
Told the ladies,
Because
He was kind.

'I'm keeping
An eye on you,
D'you mind?'
He said.

They downed
Their mops.
He never
Understood.

UNDERCLASS TO FRITH STREET

How hard and cruel it had been
When on a winter's afternoon
Her new dad got a leg across
And wounded little Jacqueline.

Though barely in her fifteenth year
Her mother said she was a slut
And threw her out 'and don't come back'
So she was taken into care.

She got away after a bit
And headed for the London lights
Together with another girl
Who knew of space in a bed-sit.

She cleaned the floors for Marks and Sparks
And hoped there was some more to life
Her friend who modelled one day said
She thought there was a job at Starks.

Her interview was very short
A little man just like her dad
He said, "Try this,' and 'Can you dance?
I don't suppose you have been taught.'

He told her she could join the crew
'And here's the money for a day
Your name is Honey from now on
And Virgy'll tell you what to do.'

She worked and saved, she understood
And in two years that seemed like ten
She'd stripped a dozen times a day
And helped her man as best she could.

Now all she dreamed of was her Bob
The son of Joe who paid the cash
He said he wanted her as wife
When he had got his steady job.

A not unhappy Jacqueline
She thought of kiddies and all that
A thick-pile carpet and a suite
He promised her when she's eighteen.

He brought some news, vile news, one day
It was her great love Bobbie's chance
An Arab prince - a week
Ten thousand pounds he said he'd pay.

She'd stayed away from easy cash
For Bobbie, he had kept he straight
and now, he could not ask her this
If he loved her and was not trash.

She said that she would do it 'Yes'
She moved into a Mayfair flat
She was alone on the first night
And cried alound in her distress.

Then Abdul came - a rainy day
It was quite early after lunch
And he was talking business things
With men who later went away.

At six o'clock she heard a knock
Soft on her brassy bedroom door
He smiled and said, "Hello, hello.'
And put his key into the lock.

He entered. She looked grey and grim
And told him she was not for sale
He then assured her that her Bob
Had said that she would sleep with him.

He ordered dinner in the flat
It was Champagne and lamby stew
With music on the new tape deck
He said he was a diplomat.

She blinked and did not grumble more
And ate and drank relaxed and laughed
And even sang a little song
And stripped as she'd not stripped before.

He threw her hundred dollar bills
Against each veil as it fell off
And then he rose and said to her
That none had given him such thrills.

She smiled so wide he held her fast
Her free hand then picked up a knife
She planted it into his back
And watched him gasp and breath his last.

Time passed and she began to sob
And dialled nine three times - 'police'
'Your name' they asked and still she sobbed
'I am the love of Maltese Bob.'

It seems they could not recognise
The gentle Conti Sant
Lying in the pool of his own blood,
The flow that ran from feudal days
Continuous in Malta's realm
Was blasted, spilt
And splattered in the mud.
In the mud of the castello
That is known as Zamitello
The spirit of the count now hovers still,
A cordial little hummer
Stays for St Martin's summer
And turns the Mġarr heat to Mġarr chill.

JANET

He waited,
She wondered,
Not long;
She'd be sixteen for all that it meant

He told her,
She gladdened,
Until;
She had reached the age of consent

He gave,
She thought,
But he took;
He took and he told her a lie

She dreamt,
Such a dream,
For a while;
Then woke up and was ready to die.

VARIATIONS ON FOUR THEMES
OR
FACETS FROM THE LIFE AND ENCOUNTERS OF ONE
KEN HILLS LABOURER

Scene One: ON THE LAND

My plot of land is coarse and wide,
The browning plow and steamy pair,
With all their strength, that's all they can,
They give in trust to me, their man.

My farrows winding deep and strait,
They skirt a path to Ye Old Gate,
The acres wait one, two, three, four,
With miles and miles of bump and heave
And still too far from the pub door.

'C'mon me lovlies soon we'll leave,
Sweat and play and tire me too,
I'll tell ye when y'er work'll do.'

And when it's ended dusk is nigh,
More other fields must need a run
For we could work until we die,
But yonder's someone else's fun.

Scene Two: ON THE ROAD

'Get going' 'orse - ye can't be tired,
This beaut'ful day lies ahead o' ye,
There's long waiting miles that are for treckin',
And I'll not stand 'round for any checkin',
So get on there and on y'er way,
Now pull if I ask - do as I say.

Round hill and dingle - right rural ride,
We'll scour each bit o' the countryside,
P'raps we" pick the hop and then,
Take some coin into the fen ,
And there I'll find her in repose,
My darling dearest buring Rose,
She'll sing for me and then she'll dance,
And flash at me her gipsy glance,
And round and round the blowing fire,
I'll look and hope and think desire,
Then I shall yearn for gold as never,
Yea, all for me and 'er forever.
'C'mon 'orse - head on my fate,
This Ken's movin' and won't be late.

Scene Three: TECHNICAL SERVICES

I drive rubbish out of town,
Me and two men also here,
My name's Hills, there's Smith and Brown,
And we're mainly in low gear.
We're off and away to mansions great,
And paltry houses plenty,
And the facts of life we carry in state,
For the lowly and the gentry.

It's always the same, and the route is our life
The Foreman's upset and the Councillor's wife
Said, 'Your men have a kind of half-mocking way.'
So we missed all her rubbish and drove on today.
'You're a dopey lot', he cries once again,
So he gets our look of suffering pain,
Then he points his finger, old Scrooge does to say,
'Come end of week you'll want your pay.'

Now we're off again and bunting's come out,
And it's waiting all stenchy and dirty,
There's egg-shell and peel, some glass and a shout
And these men start getting shirty.
A lady's complaining we've damaged her bin,
'Sorry m'love it's too big for the round.'
There's a dog over there with a great panting grin,
We're all running late and pooped good and sound.

'Wot's got 'ere Missus this ain't the bog,
Pong's enough to start a fog.'
'Have a cup with Millie Slater,
Brown and Hills can come back later!'
'Where's y'er Bert then Granny Anne,
'as 'e met y'er fancy man?'
'Ge'rr on y're cheeky lot y'know
Oi'm the one what pays y'dough.'

The cart has slowed and climbs away,
Compressed and ready for the dump,
The tipman's moves sink in decay,
Amid the sound of constant flump.
He now berates and loathes his lot,
And thinks we've hidden costly things,
And I suppose he knows it's not,
The first pick of the new gettings.

I drop into a turgid scum,
Unfastening a hard-earned hoard,
And Smith and Brown have found a plum,
And I've a share which they have stored,
The depot first, then home to rest,
The wife begins to holler,
She draws a bath and says in jest,
'I'm married to a wallah!'

Scene Four: IN THE GARDEN

Into the garden shed, no rain,
'barrow, forks and hoe again,
Mower's lost its spark once more,
Spring has endless work in store,
Borders, weeds and rubbish-lawns,
And my bank is full of thorns.

Forgive me Lord your Spring is good,
The sky is singing full of birds,
The light is shining through the wood,
And young are born to flocks and herds.

Shine hot sun on my old back,
Make up for the months of slack,
Garden seat you need some paint,
I smoke a bit and half feel faint,
And then I rest in the shed shade,
And think of things while I have strayed:
There stands a house that's fit for God,
And who on earth, what human clod,
Would want to build this place if he
Had thoughts about eternity?
I must get on - my trowel - where?
I know - I'm sure - it was, just, there!
Ah now good Lord, send us new flowers,
So we can hope and bless thy powers,
And give more strength and keep from ills,
Your humble servant, me, Ken Hills.

Benet Tredyter it was,
I heard the name and wrote it down
Lest I forget,
And then tried sleep again
And all was peace, until,
I met this stranger in another dream.

The Vicar of St Jakob's had a dream,
And ran fast from his house into the church,
And risking that his people think him mad,
He ordered everyone into the street,
And this is true, reported in the Times next day.
His church fell down;
The faithful saved;
The cavern underneath digested all;
And what had been a place of praise from mediaeval times
Fell into rubble killing nested birds
And one black cat.

My Grandma Cola also had a dream
Which came again and worried her those many years ago,
She saw a woman of the bourgeoisie
Repeat 'Anna Maria Chiusi' in the drawing-room;
Standing by the prie-dieu looking hard,
Beckoning perhaps, who knows?
Neither did the notaries who searched
Past owners of the house and genealogy
Find whom she was, nor priests discover why
She came again, but said requiems for her
That she might rest for evermore
And not frequent the dreams of Grandma Cola.

O Benet Tredyter did you
Taunt me at night to tell me what?
Need me and find you could not say more than your name?
Dear Grandma Cola - long gone now -
Was birthmarked on her ear, very small,
And if one knew one saw it,
I remember
No one had it,
Only,
She and I.

NAPLES

Shiny hot bucket-washed terraces;
Tinkly inebriating sunsets;
Pinnacles and domes still fresh
With mirror gilt on old white marble;
Walls and floors fermenting
With the rash seed of millennia;
Ardour wild and freely fertilised,
Never-ceasing wonder - so:
Breathe on you careless product of the bay;
Your stench and cockles mix with laundry
In a revelry of canticle and song,
Where Beniamino Giglis and Carusos
Add their living genius to the masterpieces
Of your cluttered baroque streets;
Where litanies of unremembered saints
Whose laughs and cries and fostered ecstasy
Begat this unremitting festival;
Where sanctity and fraud
Could place a weary head
On the lovely ample breast
Of great Leviathan,
Not old Vesuvius,
But buxom strong and kneading Mamma Mia,
Adored loved, obeyed and cherished,
With gallant San Gennaro watching always,
And when his blood does boil
Again, again, again on sunny days,
It only tells his dear beloved
No impending doom awaits,
Nor is there any cause
To stop the laughter.

Sing! sing away
O lovely Napoli
In praise of love;
And lovely fishwives,
Cry and shout!
And lazzaroni from the slums
Go! spawn the muses
That will take away the breath
Of all the world.

O Napoli!
Great contender, not for me the East;
What is Constantinople after you
O finest sight of all Europa's charm?
Did not the Greeks perceive,
And Rome Imperial too
Your quality?
O ever-lying, fornicating
Vile, unfaithful, happy wretches,
Lovers of that senseless king from Spain
You gave him back a foreign throne,
Destroyed the intelligentsia
And all the revolution it could mount,
By using whores and jettatori
And strong wine to cast oblivion
On an obfuscated, fascinated enemy;
And those that did not suffer from a pox,
Or die for no apparent reason,
You knifed discreetly in dark alleyways
That Ferdinando might stay on
To see with you his fresh-caught catch of fish,
And sometimes deficate to cheering and applause.
And so he filled his great and royal barge
With bandsmen, flutes, violas,
Countertenors, mandolins,

To serenade an orange-blossom
Scented smiling fond Lucia,
Or even such an English rose
As Emma Hamilton.

O Napoli,
Your viceroys and your kings,
Have passed away,
But you live on like old Vesuvius,
Pizza, vino, spaghetti, amore
The gran' preservatore del fascino,
Mano cornuta,
O Sole Mio, Luna e Bella,
tarantella,
Cor'ngrata and Catari
Serena mia can't you see?
The crust is very thin today;
The craters rumble more.
Che m'nimporta a me,
Non c'è che fa'
I tango for amore.
Today my love is Carmelina
Tomorrow perhaps Teresina
My heart sings from my mandolina
while Doom makes love to Destiny.

O Napule!
Niende vuglia di lavura',
Malincunia,
Sotto 's't balcuncinu moriro'
Per la donna bruna.
You wanna see Pompeii, yes sir?
Che n'dici 'ste parule amare?
I do anything for you my lady

Look Happy!
Peppino will be your lover.
Una serenata?
I sing this one for you;
You are my bella, bella, bella.
Me, the guide of King George, Eisenhower;
Eh ... cardinali ... my friends;
Zi Teres, frutta di mar, pesch',
Furmaggi, chitarre, manduline.
There is munasterio e Santa Chiara,
Quante femmine che ci su!
Quante femmine sincere!
Your tip save my family;
Razza di merda!
Carmelina baffutina
Dammi un gran' bacon',
Va bene morirò.

O lovely Napoli
Go! spawn the muses
That will take away the breath
Of all the world.

BY THE ARNO

She looked down from her parapet
and sipped a gin and orange, pink
and powdery was life as people walked
below and she remembered.

Aunt Elsie was my favourite,
unparalleled, a confidante.
"I'm now a porter at the Tate," I said,
"and if one's interested in trends
and what men will create, where better?"

Her rough accomplished voice and teeth
all gilded in another age
emerged
and told me all
about a picture,
"John Singer Sargent:
your Uncle never knew."

Mandated, I returned to claim
a parcel neatly wrapped in brown
and stained a little, sealed
at Mayfair's Coutts
with bluish wax
and old white ribbon.

In a seventh story flat
I fretfully unpacked the gift:
Aunt Elsie's pink cherubic skin,
her golden locks, the youthful cheeks
of her behind, an ostrich feather
in her hand and come-on-hither
fluffy features soft indented
by some vulcan god, a carnal homage
to the deity of love I see;
and in the distance, pines,
the Arno, a campanile
and a dome.

Aunt Elsie's what?
Aunt Elsie's dead!
The telegram is lying
flat - it sings
a dirge,
and I
the only one
to give response.

A plan dawns
and then takes shape,
to hang my dear Aunt Elsie
to the Tate.

We carry her so stealthily
on such a day as few would choose to visit,
and I, with Joe and Fred
(colleagues)
unseen,
place her by a Whistler
in Gallery XIII.

They splash Aunt Elsie in the press
and hail the Keepr's wisdom. Bliss!
(he'll show her, "For a month or so.")
and far from being petty,
makes arrangements and agrees
to lend her to the Getty.

Have a tea with me my dear;
Piace il tè? We drink it here;
This is Florence - not like Rome;
Not like Italy - like home.
It is good for you: I made
A small cake with marmalade.
Call me Ida - fill your plate;
Not Marchesa! - It's my fate,
Now Landini Scott Filgate.
I unmarried Sachetti Profumi
Do you remember? when you last knew me.

We went to a party and danced all the night;
We were still dancing when it became light;
Manfredi he kissed me - yes, and Marcello;
But when it was you it was the più bello.

Can I forget what you said then to me?
"Oh Ida I've promised and cannot be free
Oh damn damn the spring time in Kent o my dove
I can't leave the firm and marry for love."

Marcello he had a great villa not far;
And Manfredi he drove in that wonderful car;
E Giorgio ... my mother she said that maybe;
Then you went away - and so it was he ...

Now please will you have one more cup of tea?

A sidelong glance past Kemble
Before five valleys meet,
A Gucci scarf around her neck.
She looked superior in her seat
(No Smoking in the Second Class).
Her face in profile looked away,
I sniffed her scent but only just,
And saw her minute signet ring
Beside my Times and felt I must
Observe her eyes, her nose her lips,
This aphrodite's little face.
But time had ticked away so fast,
Too soon the brakes slowed down our pace.
Her hand moved onto my arm-rest
As my divinity turned round
And it was not as I had thought
My fancy'd not surmised this cloud
And both of us got off at Stroud.

Into the street and right along
The shopping precinct's window panes,
In cold and slushy Cotswold March
The Light of India wafts its scent
To tantalise and find desire.
I entered almost in a swoon,
To chicken scents of evensong,
And blissful mists of vindaloo,
Nan, bhagi and lime pickle.
Here a haven - ah Madras
Tandoori and the sizzlers flirt
To gorge full-bodied appetites,
The old imperial quest
Of aromatic spices found,
With orientalish delight,
In Middle Street in Stroud.

THE BULL

George, you lived with all the cows,
No yolk for you,
Just pastures, meadows,
Praise, applause,
All for your appetite,
How trite.

Yet you too ran out of steam,
And died today,
Your carcass slimped, arcane,
While, passers by, your cows,
O dear,
Quite unaware.

THERE HE LIES

My very own and dearest miscreant,
There he lies,
The striver,
The stirrer,
The ever-blind intruder,
The realist unconscious,
The pleasure wager,
There he lies,
There is no longer a person peresent in his body.

THE POINT OF NO RETURN

The point of no return
came one day early,
    The point of no return
is in the mist,
    The way of now today
is lost since last Setpember,
    But which September
which September have I missed?

EXIT

Those useful reserves had dwindled away,
And winter seemed destined to take its hard toll,
The manager wanted a 'state of affairs',
And we went away to a sunny resort.

Campari and Coke the umbrellas proclaimed,
Caroline looked remarkably white,
She had lobster and conch, I had the same,
And siestas that lasted well into the night.

Our terrace for dinner was perfect, so calm,
The moon on the sea and the balm of the palm,
For only a week - but what cares were there now?
'It's the telephone sir,' he said with a bow.

It was 'Darling my dear, where on earth have you been?'
Had we sold all our shares? Of course it was Jean?
Did I know that the market had rallied and soared
And she was feeling incredibly bored?

'I've got tickets,' she said, oh the miserable brute!
With Alfie as well - they'd soon be en route.
'We arrive in the morning, at six, make a note.'
My Dolce Amaro stuck in my throat.

As my heart fell smack like an egg from its nest,
I thought of my woes and I thought of my rest,
Then I cried, oh the pain, as she said with delight,
'Would you mind awfully meeting the flight?'

Your Grace, in haste,
I checked on twenty saints who died by drowning
in river and sea
most of them male
whereas
your painting's
of a girl.

Of the women, seven virgins
all thrown into the sea
in a group in AD 304
Yours is not of them.

St Maxima
drowned,
with her husband though,
in Pannonia,
this does not fit.

St Godelieva,
1070 from Boulogne,
the costume's wrong,
unlikely.

St Zoe, well,
converted by Sebastian,
AD 286 probably not
the detail's wrong again.

St Antonina,
4th century,
drowned
in a sack or a barrel,
no.

St Rufina, I think
perhaps,
AD 257,
feast day July 10th,
thrown into the Tiber
tied to a stone
same as in Your Grace's picture.

HAIKU

Bleach-thin yellow silk
hanging loose along long walls
breathing unconscious.

Paler than pear pulp
abstracting silent numbness
fermented by love.

Cast my eyes on reams
of slowly fainting lilies
wisping into white.

Fragrance and fresh fruit
papaya, mango, lemon,
gee and tee for two.

Wispy lispy love
tread upon my aching heart
now and now and then.

Hot rocks of St Paul's
scalding in the midday sun
mobs of volunteers.

Festive cool water
embracing pink protrusions
calm and deep and blue.

Guilty goddesses
your bathing costumes do not
hide the rest of you.

Love matters the most
it can smile and cry and die
And live forever.

Saintliness is art
my love was a work of art
not a saint at all.

Hold my hand today
go away tomorrow please
do not come again.

Marble slabs of life
embellished, shiny side up
otherwise grim.

Have you tasted all?
I have tasted all there is
bitter-sweet is best.

THE UNIVERSE

The Universe was solid yesterday
from a million billion trillions
breathes a blasted fragment
where Art
and Death
hold heavy hands.

Should the heart-string's tug still linger,
Should, I hope: there I would be,
Where the luzzu's catch lampuki,
In a blue September sea,
Where the dins are called 'papali',
When there's festa and mortali,
Frescoed candles, silver plate,
And the children stay up late,
And a vara-like Karmena,
And Marie and Ġiuseppina,
And their friends Susanne and Doris,
Ta' Karmelu and Tonina,
Spending golden days tal-festi,
Wearing white and some ċelesti,
Shorn of all their black and grey,
Who will walk with them today?
O Dun Anġ quote santi padri,
"Dixit Paulus alle madri
'Oxores obdete semper.'
O what pressure has thy temper!
What it is to wax so lyric,
Bless they solemn panegyric,
Make crescendi grandi, forti,
Soon, so soon shall we be morti,
Damnatione, carne vale,
Viva Malta spirituale!
Hear the clamour in the piazza,
Ġelati and te fit-tazza,
And qubbajt ta' Wenz Abdilla,
And the Banda ta' l-Istilla,
and Maestro Aquilina,
Playing 'Forza Ancor Ċensina'.
Great St Paul and La Valette,
Passeġġiata Marsamxett,
Pastizzi, Pintu Grand Master,
The heart beats a little faster.
Puliti mostly kuġini,
Katterin is a hannini.

Pastazzati from the harbours,
Spring and orange-blossom arbours,
Oh the scent of Casal Lija,
Arum lilies, bougainvillaea,
Carob trees and, frot tat-tina,
The palazzi of Mdina,
Dragonara noble mesne,
Fennel-scented San Martin,
Those mnarijas at Verdala,
Pines and rabbit and the għanja.
Are there races still at Marsa?
No Ghirlando in a farsa?
Oh the Manoel how sublime
Horses Necks during half time
And what style the old parati?
Il madoffi kemm ksuħati,
Freddy Gollcher? Reynaud gone?
Sur Tonin? Zizu Randon?
Is Pike quoted still today?
And the lift is gone away?
Żażu, Pawlu it-Tork, all those?
Marie, John, Sandru ... repose?
Edwin, Frank, Austin and George?
Caruanell and Ettie Borg?
Hannibal, Bajama too,
Yes I knew Saverinu.
Uncle Pep, Gonzi and Mabel,
Lie beneath their marble label.
O baħar abjad, majjistral,
Riħ isfel and il-grigal,
Sant Irmu and ħobż biż-żejt,
It-Torok, marelli gate,
Antiporta, imfietaħ kbar,
Karrozzin, ġbejniet tal-bżar,
Timpana and pastizzot,
Karawett, ħalib tal-bot
Living, dead: oh bound or free,
Far away across the sea,
You are always part of me
O blessed blessed Malta.

RETURN TO STAGNO

My past climbed the open stairs,
Spring water ran below and geese,
The scent of bakery relived
The memory of long ago.

The ancient door waited unlocked,
Till sun lit ceded halls,
Beneath high muscled stretching beams
Dark frescoes celebrated fame.

The niche smiled, waved, I bowed
Into the aromatic smoke,
And every thing I saw I knew,
And the small bell tolled.

I heard a slow Te Deum ring,
And I was home forever now,
Home to retreat to orange shade,
And peel the fruit eternally.

PRINCESS

Poutiatine O Poutiatine
It was nineteen seventeen
And you wore a kapellin,

Admirals and rampollini,
Benestanti, poverini,
Made up any good excuse
To see you in the Ballet Russe,
To see you as the Swan Princess,
To see you - slender, a caress,
A-glimmer, white, in your tutu,
Inflamed or veiled or sombre you,
You, you, for you their hidden sighs,
Disguised, the ardour in their eyes,
'till you performed the fouetté
And women sank or said, 'How dare ...'
(And still she spun those fairy thighs
Until the tension reached the skies).
O gipsy girl, O heroine,
What passion in a tamborine!
The chandelier, perhaps the roof
A-quiver, shiver. Yet aloof
You polished maid of noble poses,
They flooded all your stage with roses.

ET CREDIS CINERES CURARE SEPULTOS
(And do you believe that the buried ashes care)

Still, I shall dream beneath this earth,
And hear the song of the Merill,
And see l'ingliża and busbiez,
A speckled rock, thorns and harrub,
And floating fronds shorn from the palm,
Far out upon the blackest sea,
Where Karabużu's ċimi float,
Alone along a rounded sky,
Then the tunnaċ is being caught,
Some trill, lampuki, a ħanżir,
And God is praised, 'O Alla kbir',
A ċerviola looks like gold,
And as the sun descends and fades,
And homeward bound are all the boats,
The gabilotti's mules and goats,
Are neighing as they settle in,
And fenek-dogs like Pharaoh's hounds,
Brown-eyed are sniffing at the cat,
And lamps glow in the streets with steps,
Those leading from the harbour shores,
Where life goes on, on board, in bars,
Until the lights have faded out,
A distant bell; a hidden shout,
A darkened day is gone to rest,
And all is spent until:
The spirit moves across the land,
The heart, the ashes understand,
It is quite warm, it is quite warm,
For they belong and love lives on.

IN AFFECTIONATE TRIBUTE
TO THE SINGLEMINDEDNESS OF
MONSIGNOR JOSEPH APAP BOLOGNA NAVARRA CASSIA
WHO SAILED A STRAIGHT COURSE INTO THE ETHEREAL

She ebbed away, this earthly life,
Commencing her great flight abroad,
And came upon a place through which,
Pass all of those whom Earth have trod,
The great, the weak, the wise, the bold,
The users and the used,
They take a path as fits the want,
Until is reached the vital end.

Upon her road she walked alone,
She saw her past in squandered time,
And slowly now she journeyed on,
And gaped aghast at all her deeds,
The portent of her span and task.

The truth it shrieked in blatant shape,
Shone out in light and brightness cold,
And mantling her in strength found new,
In bursting love, she braced herself,
She cried for joy in ardent plaint,
She cried aloud her endless need,
And stretched her arms into the glare.

MARIE

Who's to write of dear Marie
Who described our life so well
And a great big do, and tea,
And a happy wedding bell?
Passing time and memory dull;
To the album - shed a tear,
I can read, and see, and hear.

Who's to write of dear Marie,
Who'll remember her in rhyme,
Should one use 'o'er thou' and 'thee',
Draw in words the summertime,
Should one tell of her sweet smile?
Is it all for naught to try:
How she lived prepared to die?

Then who's to write of dear Marie,
Who's the one to praise her well?
Could I? No but only she
Should reflect her words and tell
Something of the writer who
Saw the bloom and sky and sea,
And told her maker it was He.

Adieu
Adieu
And rest Marie.

Mother of mine
  Move slowly today
  I'll tell you about
  The season's been long
  Cold ambling it goes
  Dark to proceed on the way

Mother of mine
  Stay for me still
  Far is the sight
  Of sun-smattered grain
  Set are the eyes
  Of an old man in pain
  Cutting's the work
  And blunt is the gain

Mother of mine
  Turn back come look here
  Is even the Spring for you wait
  Love bursts unbroken
  To live now and on
  Master of the nagging load
  Of time beneath the snow
  And dark in God's only rays.

MABEL

Miss Strickland
You were born too soon
To rouse the men of Malta
And their appendages
From their ancient habits;

You thought you could extend
The legend lately lost
Through bluster, faith and courage
And that you could ignore
The great impediment;

Denied by maidenhood
Deferred by fobs
Debarred from access
Deterred by fate
Denied;

And so it stayed
Until one day
A day that's gone
Now who will ever be
Another Mabel.

LINES EVOKING NOT ONLY THE MEMORY
BUT ALSO THE TIMES
THROUGH WHICH PASSED
SYMBOLICALLY, COMPLACENT, POLITE AND FAITHFUL
THE NOBLE TERESINA TRAPANI GALEA FERIOL
DEI BARONI DI SAN MARCIANO

O Teresina you are gone
Nymphet of the Belle Epoque
And a gay jeunesse dorée
Thé-dansants and grandes soirées
Gardens of the great and high
Follies lit in the night sky
And Baron Azopardi's balls
And carnivals and lustrous halls
And dancing oriental foes
And cavaliers and dominos
And monsigneural silver plate
And balconies and village fêtes
Un atto di presenza
Piacere della cognoscenza
Respect, virtue and compliance
Honour and a good alliance
A young daughter's wistful cry
An aspiration and a sigh
The need to call a notary
God preserve the noble coterie
In the libro d'oro found
All secure and safely bound
All the canons kept intact
Did you think about the pact?
Did you cogitate and wonder
Could it all be torn asunder?
While and years rolled on and more
Did Louis Quinze become a bore?

When the bombs finally came
Did you go on just the same?
When the farmers did not bow
Did you ask yourself why? how?
All those tenants, no respect
Why were they the new elect?
Oh the rent act, income tax
Morals now so very lax
While things crumbled into dust
Was there no one you could trust?
Was there not some champion stud?
Could you not revive the blood?
Weren't they made of sterner stuff?
Past and gone - a little puff?
Had they not bred you for caste?
Did you know you were the last?

A SPECIAL PERSON

When I think of bright Spring flowers
I do not think of you,
When I brood on my desires,
Jolly on and muddle through,
Wager fate or miss the act,
Hear the bells, nostalgic, ringing,
Dance with Bacchus through the night,
Blame the world for a bad joke,
Feel convinced my strength is utter,
Disappoint, distress, delight,
Make the peace or start the fraction,
Promise all my credit holds,
Take on stress or volunteer,
Die of laughter or ennui
I do not think of you.

In my life you feature subtly,
Deeply though, and far away
Laughter rings in Tuscany,
Somerset when I was young,
On the beach at St Paul's Bay;
Part of me you are that fosters,
In my heart, something not faint,
Rousing, safe and reassuring.
Should I reckon on the day
Fate decides you go away,
I would think of youth and lunches,
Grosvenor Street in the old club,
A first bike at Cuerden Hall,
Eggs you sent a child at school,
What was dared in Gloucestershire,
Look around the empty spaces,
Feel the void and start to weigh
The few things I care to count.

You shouted D.D.I. come here,
You shouted fucking D.D.I.,
Your voice boomed raucous through the heat
Left, left, let's show 'em who we are.

You swelled our chests with pride at last,
Your eyes betrayed the slightest smile,
You marched us on and on and on
Until we died:

We died of pride, we showed 'em too,
We puffed our fags and laughed,
The beer tasted better now
Because of you. Good-bye old Fra.

DIES IRAE

When my obituary is written,
They're bound to get it wrong,
They'd never write 'A hypocrite'
Of how I far preferred music, poetry, the arts,
To having dinner
With financial friends
Whose aspirations moved me less
Than their superlatives
And choiceless adjectives.
When I tired
How I smiled while people waffled on
To try and hide distraction,
Then felt a little sorry for their dye-cast lots,
Because they knew no muse.

How much I loved the old religion,
How partial I was to Kees van Dongen,
Longhi, Manzu, Emilio Greco,
How I wanted to live in a house
Full of naïves,
Where bread was baked
In the courtyard rooms,
And cook was fat,
And threw things to the dog and cat,
Fed everyone,
And spoilt the young.
How my dream of bliss
Was sitting under trellised vines
With wives and children, mothers, fathers,
In-laws, cousins, and a cleric or two,
Baroque, the sea and aunts.

How, if I could, I should, I know
I would have well indulged myself
And had my own soprano always there,
Whose trills,
With olives, pasta, oil and fresh tomatoes,
Would rouse more passion in the heart of me
Than dreams of youth, of fantasy, of odalisques,
Of wild ambitions, power, honours and such-life.

'He leaves to mourn his loss', they'd say,
And talk about a 'Celebration' of his life,
But not for me, this 'Celebration' -
Please, hold back.,
I need a Dies Irae,
Black,
And my soprano reaching those orgasmic notes
To open up my Heaven wide,
With choral Requiescats,
Booming Sempiternums,
And lasting Seculas
And Seculorums.

THE BOSOM OF VIRTUE

There is prima facie evidence
Professor Knox said more than once
But one cannot be quite sure
We must measure and make tests
The issue concerns a passage
Both traditional and symbolic
Below the legs of Prudence
Meandering diagonally
Towards the finger of Virtue
Holding subliminal configuration
Of the corporeal aspect.
What I see is the cross-figurative
Balance being central to the allegory
Virtue carrying a symbol spear
Her finger pointing high
Wards off Temptation.
We have free-painted shadow areas
Clearly discernable half tones
And a clear congruence
Due to the rococo palace
Trapezium library fitting the canvas
In the complementary cavity
Of its wild soffit.
The asymmetry engendered an urge
In the artist I maintain
To disqualify the reality of architecture
Through the assonance of his brush
Thereby compensating the shorter parallel.
He achieved this by disaccentuating
The irregularity of the perpendiculars
Through tension, urgency and emphasis
All embodied in the elongated strength
Of the bosom of Virtue,
You understand.

COLORATURA
(Darling love me now and come to me)

Da,a,a,a,
ling;
li,ie ie ie ie,
a:
ie ie ing.
la-a-a-a,
ver er;
me ie, ie, ie,
ie-ie-ie-ie-ie-ie-ie,
ver er, er
meeeeeeeeeeeeeeeeeee,
na;
a, a, a, a, a,
a-a-a-a-a-a
ah; ow:
la ver me
na a a;
a now
a and car,
a and car,
a and ca a a a a;
a:
aaaaaaaaaaaaaaaaaaa
arm
to:
mi ie ie
to mi ie ie
ie-ie-ie-ie-ie-ie
ie:
ie.

THREE TRIOLETS

She sat in a chair
I sat on the table
I just had to stare
She sat in a chair
O what did I care
If I felt unstable
She sat in a chair
I sat on the table

I'd asked her to dance
She said I'm not able
I'd taken a chance
I'd asked her to dance
She gave me a glance
This soft dreamy sable
I'd asked her to dance
She said I'm not able

I think I shall leave
And move from this table
It's hard to believe
I think I shall leave
This daughter of Eve
She said I'm not able
I think I shall leave
And move from this table

Andronicus had no conception of manners
Because his upbringing was a pastiche
Concerning itself only with rights and claims
Declining a fair estimation of any form or
Edifying standard or even erudition
Fermenting a never-ending aggression
Governed by lusting after victory
Here and plunder there
Intent and dominion
Justified by strength and power
Killing any concept of civilised
Leniency or even truce
Merely a weakness to be regretted
Never to be emulated or accepted
Or vaguely contemplated
Perhaps within the family
Quaint notion, no, never
Respond with weakness
Sever all connection and fight
True to the aspiration
Under no circumstances bend
Valour or vision
With wandering thoughts of tired forebearance
Xenodochy is not for Alexanders
Yesterday is not a dream for warriors
Zeniths come to ardent causes only.

I AM A

I am a
I am
I
am I
am I a
my
am
a am I
am a I
I a am
my am
a a
a am
a I.

I was in love
I thought I was in love
I thought I was in love with you my dear
I was I thought in love
I was
I was with you
I thought I was
I thought with you
I was I thought
I thought with you
I thought I was my dear
I was I thought my dear
I thought in love
I was my dear
I thought.

TRIOLETS

Remember Canoodles
Our first luncheon date
In April at Boodles
Remember Canoodles
Pall Mall with your poodles
How perfect our fate
Remember Canoodles
Our first luncheon date.

I love you Louise
By day and by night
Please, please, please, please,
I love you Louise
Come put me at ease
My tender delight
I love you Louise
By day and by night

O darling Elaine
Your mind has me ravaged
You drive me insane
O darling Elaine
Come kiss me again
I'm ethereally savaged
O darling Elaine
Your mind has me ravaged

She gave me the shove
I'd nothing to give
She found a new love
She gave me the shove
My own little dove
She said oh you'll live
She gave me the shove
I'd nothing to give.

He gave up the cloth
O fearful disclaimer
He'd plighted his troth
He gave up the cloth
In partisan froth
Came his no-bomb exclaimer
He gave up the cloth
O fearful disclaimer.

Mrs Grima's Tontis
Are the finest I have seen,
They span the realms of fantasy,
In pastel-coloured sheen,
The scope of their perspective
Is enticingly displayed,
As in the lamplight or the sun
They stand up unafraid.
I've tried to fault them all in vain
And touched upon each detail there,
Whose nuances transcend an age
They are the very finest pair.

* Egidio Tonti was an Italian artist who painted in Malta in
the 1920s.

1.   I am Mario Sant dei Conti
      Nava Bres Moroni Tanti
      Only son that did accrue
      To the late Saverinu
      And Consiglia Camenzuli
      Saintly wife of ten years truly
      Nephew, heir or tantamount
      To the celibate old Count
      Vox majorem non c'e male
      Son erede universale.

2.   I am Rita Camilleri
      My mother is a Mifsud Fleri
      I'm half engaged to Mario Sant
      He's forty-two and won't confront
      The question of our making ties
      I wonder if he's telling lies
      He says he wants to marry me
      But fears that with my pedigree
      His uncle the old Count Simone
      May not approve of our unione.

3.   I am the widow Camilleri
      Mother of Rita (my little fairy)
      A daughter innocent of blame
      She will and shall take on the name
      Sant dei Conti Nava Bres
      Moroni Tanti; none the less
      I cannot always remain dumb
      It's vi o va and the outsome
      Will bring rejoicing or great woe
      To the Conte I must go.

4.   I am the Conte, can you see
That I'm nearly eighty-three?
I feel strong and full of life
I could even take a wife!
Who's that waiting in the hall?
It's a lady fair and tall.
Says it's Mrs Camilleri?
Oh Elvira Mifsud Fleri!.
What! My nephew and her daughter?
Who told him that he could court her?

5.   I am Grezz of Wied-Gremxula
An old maid, but he can't fool her
Fifty years in this palazzo
Looking after that ragazzo.
I shall warn the good Consiglia
Here she comes in her pariglia
Come to pay respects - the dear
Ooo - she has a lot to hear!
She will tell the Monsignor
He must know - I shall make sure.

6.   I am the widow of Saverin
Here to do my duty, seen
By the people in the piazza
Dressed in black on my terrazza
In church daily on my chair
Oh good doctors are so rare
I have brought Conte Simone
Some more honey and lampone
It should help his wheezy chest
He says I know what is best.

7.   I am the Canon Calcedonio
     Youngest son of Conte Antonio
     Brother of the present Count
     Under pressure as a fount
     Of knowledge for the use of many
     To give advice if I have any
     I live off meagre Spadafora
     The benefice of Zia Cora
     I'm not the greatest theologue
     But I get on well with the underdog.

O Marquis Scicluna thou beacon of light,
How strong is thine armour! How gallant thy plight!
Thy chest swells colossal, thy guns and thy swords
Are championed by tenants and well 'scutcheoned
broads.
'Smite death on ye varlets!' 'tis only ablution,
When feudal Lord Joseph strikes down revolution.
The Baron, the Marquis, the Duke Joe Scicluna,
Has part of his arsenal hid on Kemmuna,
And more in his dungeons, Madliena and Fgura,
Where peasants keep watch from his ġiren and ħbula.
Gadroons at the palace and gold mirrored halls,
A site fit for sovereigns and sumptuous balls;
And the marble symbolic is huge without sever,
That the House of Scicluna should live on forever.
O the flickers of light are resplendent in or,
And in glass chandeliers where the crystal is pure,
And beneath stands the Marquis, his hand on his
heart,
His cavalier cape and his tall boots apart,
His medals and orders are gleaming and bright,
His bows and his charm are the cause of delight,
His fingers they click, and the orchestra plays,
As in a good dream of forgotten days.
God bless the Marquis! So goes the xandir,
Pay him his homage and get a parir,
'Markis x'se naghmel serqitni din Ċetta?'
'Qeghda fit-torri u ġiebli iċ-ċavetta.'
'Markiz għandi borża deheb ġol kexxun,'
'Ġib kollox il-bank, mela inti miġnun?'
But the bank went away in a pilfering storm,
'Curse the damned vassals!' He would not conform.
In portly splendour he defended his casks,
And the beer was saved; 'Oh so many tasks!'
But the height of finesse he achieved for his clique,
When he built the suave and delighting Mystique.

From the debris of war with strange hues and odd tones,
He transformed into wonder a great pile of stones,
Where there's always some music from Bechstein his grand',
With bongos and olè! The Don Jose Band,
And El Marques, Supremo (he's also called Cisk),
Shoots a glance and a smirk at a lush odalisque,
She slides off her chaise in a rapture of grace,
A dance from the navel, half covered her face,
Her veils oriental, her pelvis a wow!
And nobody knows that she hails dear from Slough,
They call her Fatima this daughter of Kama,
Miss Jones charms the lot with her year at 'the drama',
Then banquets are served, there's a well-starched retainer,
It's Fenech Flambé and not one abstainer.
The merriment swells with guitars and olé!
The toast is none other than Marquis Jose,
'Long may he reign as the scourge of all varlets,
Raise high those glasses to The King of the Starlets, olé!'

Grand Master Pinto you were grandest of all,
Grander by far than Grand Master de Paule,
As for Verdala, indeed La Valette,
Though of the Order were not of the set.
Beyond your great presence, no, nobody shone,
No de Redin and no de Rohan,
Not a Perellos,
Not Vasconcellos.
De Clermont de Chattes Gessan one is sure
Could not compare, as could not Wignacourt;
And far too bizarry
Was the gay Zondadari;
As for Hompesch,
In his German calesche,
He had no finesse
Just like Ximenes;
And all the world knew, but who would impeach
The great Spanish lover Fra Ramon Despuig?
Jean d'Homedes!
Martino Garces!
As bad as del Ponte,
Or even del Monte.
And Lascaris Castellar
One has to debar,
If looks ossify
It was him and St Jaille;
Far better, compared, a great object d'art
Was good old Grand Master Gregorio Caraffa;
And then on a par but seulement from un angle
It is fair to include Grand Master de Sengle.
No, not La Cassiere
Nor indeed Cotoner;
And though none could trace even a little faux pas
Of Manoel, by birth The Prince Vilhena,
Noblest of all, and great in his time,
He never quite made it into the sublime.
It was you, you alone, who made the grand slam,
As the grandest of all since the great L'Isle Adam.

PURPLE BEAT

When I became a monsignor
A state I thought I could endure
Although one had to be so pure
And then have style and some allure
I had a ring of high grade or
And it was kissed by all the poor
And these I blessed and all I saw
As is prescribed by canon law
I donned my purple and felt sure
I looked so right in what I wore
I mixed with those who are secure
And these I tried to reassure
My anecdotes came by the score
Until one day my earthly store
Looked Heavenward - so to withdraw
I made a little overture
My friend the Abbot's open door
Perhaps a little sinecure
I should have thought of this before
My mattress lay on a stone floor
The cook was not a carnivore
A month and every kind of chore
I felt it was a total cure
My knees were not a little sore
My spirit rose up more and more
'twas no return - no heretofore
And so it was that I forbore
From being the old Monsignor.

TONSURE

When monsignori are no more,
And monks and priests of heretofore,
With all the nuns are coutured in disguise,
Would it not make sense if just,
Their marked coiffures became a must,
For all the world to see and recognise?

They could shed their old black habits,
They could throw their buckles out,
No more ropes and leather sandles,
Sackcloth, hair-shirts, flays and fasts,
They could send brocade and vestments,
Capes and cottas, mitres too,
Thuribles and all their crosiers,
Lace and ermine, hats and purple,
To theatrical surveyors,
And museums and sale rooms,
Silver candlesticks and relics,
Carved confessionals and thrones,
Silver pommelled baldacchinos,
and basilica umbrellas,
Altar fronts emblazoned, jewelled,
Chalices enamelled, precious,
Pect'rals, monstrances and rings,
They could shed the homage gold,
They could switch to wood and pewter,
They could love, embrace and share,
Brotherhoods with the reformed,
Then abolish heresy,
Catechism, latin chants,
With the triple crown and lent,
And all hold hands, kiss and repent,
Yet, they might think once again,
And keep something from the past,
And more committing than a collar,
Is the tonsure.

When monsignori are no more,
And monks and priests of heretofore,
With all the nuns are coutured in disguise,
Would it not make sense if just,
Their marked coiffures became a must,
For all the world to see and recognise?

ELATIO
ANDREÆ   ALBERTI
PRINCEPS
ET
MAXIMUS MAGISTER
DOMINATIO TYRANNUS
SUMMUS
ORDINIS GEROSOLIMITANO
A.D. MCMLXXXVIII
VIRTUS CLARA
AETERNAQUE HABETUR

(Virtue abides illustrious and eternal)

THE ELEVATION OF ANDREW

Andrew spoke or made a joke
In Latin, French, Tibetan too
(His Erse and Greek a trifle weak)
His Pakistani reached a peak
While twelve more tongues: a rhapsody.

He taught at school, and made one fool
Progress with such alacrity
That he could chaff at all the staff
And win most prizes by the half
And teach the organist some binary.

One of the few, and yet Andrew,
Humility resplendent,
Hid his pate, it seemed quite late
Among the knight-monks of a state
Subjected to a sovereign pastor.

Thus Andrew bowed and thus he vowed
Away his wealth and quarterings
Until they rose to apotheose
His name all glorious 'midst those
Electing him Grand Master.

PRANZO

The Falsoni Moscati
Suggested a party,
In the beautiful ġnien
Of the Marquis Fiddien,
Count della Catena
Planned the great ċena,
The service was set
By Marquis Ghajn Qajjed,
The Briffa Brincati
Lent the posati,
The Sceberrases
All the glasses,
The Oliviers
The chairs,
The Bowers
Did flowers,
Mgr dei Conti Schembri
Stood to bless the great assembly,
The Diar-il-Bniet and Buqana
Brought timpana,
Ta Sant Fournier
Consommé (clear),
The famiglia ta' Gourgun
Aljotta and muntun,
Ta Testaferrata
Qassata,
A Mr Mizzi
Pastizzi,
All the Manducas
Came with lampukas,
The Benwarrad
With pixxispad,
Marquis Scicluna
With a fekruna,

The Baron of Qlejjgħa
A chicken but nejjgħa,
Ta' Ghaxaq and Bonici
Due pernici,
The Moroni Viani
Faġiani,
Ta Chritien
Summien,
Rare and pink from the Castelletti
Came the beef in fetti fetti,
Ta' Adami
Brought salami,
Ta' Barbaro
Escargot,
And the Apap Bologni
Contorni,
The Paleologos
Tomatoes,
Ta' Delicata
Patata,
Ta' Tabone
Maccarone,
Ta' Cassar Torreggiani
Tqiq l-aktar bajdani,
The Marchese Mattei
Xej,
Ġewlaq ġbejniet
Ta de Pirijiet,
The Baron Carbot
Brought all the frot,
Except for Chapelle's
Lumiċells,
And the best of the tina
Of the Conti Messina,

The bon vini
Came from the Azopardini
And the Conte Fontani
In all ten damigiani,
Ċertu Chircop
Brought the Xirob,
Sant Manduca what a relief
Safely looped over the fief,
While Caruanell took aerial shots
Below Ganado stirred the pots
On the great tigan
Made in the garage of Sur Gasan,
Xuereb, Rizzo and Mifsud
Cooked the laham and the hut,
Helped by many braided flunkeys
Taking orders from the Bianchis,
Bella scena! Che bel parco!
All agreed with Profs Demarco,
Meli Bugeja procured the stout poles
Which Zammit Tabona placed in their holes,
Camilleri, Magri, and Galea
Raised the great flag of Italia,
Borg and Gatt managed to track
The de Trafford Union Jack,
Then the Prince of Selimbria
Laid on feu de joie,
And the Conti Sant
Feu fulminant,
Dottor Filippo Farrugia Randon
Compered from the palco with abandon
Maestro Cachia Caruana
Led the orchestra 'Nazzjon Taghna'
Now sang the Preziosi
With voci sontuosi,
Also Montalto
As contralto,
With Trigona
Biex jintona,

And Formosa
Toccando qualche cosa,
U Pullicin
Iżżomm il-ħin,
The Baron of San Marciano
Lent a piano,
Ta Stagno Navarra
A kitarra,
Bonavita
A dancer called Rita,
Ta' Budaq,
A żaqq,
Miss Delia
Played 'Allegria',
Miss Storace
A vivace,
Contino Gauci
Un cantico Għawdxi.
Xa ħadd ta' Sedley,
a medley
The Markiz de Sain
Offered souffle and rosolin,
The Baron of Tabria
Vagun ħelu from Elia,
and the Gomerini
Cioccolatini,
Biscuttini from the Englands
And figolli from the Stricklands,
The Duca Mattei
Brought café au lait,
Reynaud
Pernod,
And finally the Conte Gatto
Praised it all and said, 'Ben fatto',

E ... lo vedo'
Said one Toledo,
'Molto Bello,'
Said a Bonello,
'Si si sapessi',
Said Marquis Alessi.
Mgr Ferro covered in lace
Rose to say the final grace,
And then all the kbarat started
To bow and wave as they departed,
Off they went with noble zeal
To think about another meal.

One ate pheasant in West One
In a manner comprehensible,
Game chips, crumbs, the usual thing
One had always deemed as sensible.
In Dover Street they served this dish
In a form unrecognisable,
And in fact one felt quite brave
To set aside what seemed advisable.
The meal was served 'a l'italiano',
The menu said it was fagiano.
One tried Luigi's winey sauce,
And his Barolo spread the smiles
Across the other tables there,
While mandolins sent shudders out
Like arrows from a Cupid's bow.
One's passion rose, one felt unstable,
One reeled about the grace of Mabel.
It was her hand one touched at first,
It was the way one had been versed.
It was so strange, one felt quite free
To hold her pink and cuddly knee.
One thought of King Umberto Two,
And saw the bitter exile sink,
And dying, with his well known cry,
One felt those words and that last sigh,
   'My Florence ....
    My Rome ....
    My Naples ....
Oohhhh ....'
My soul!
My plum. My peach,
My apple-blossom,
Take me home and love me Mabel.

An haircut at Trumper's
Like a brigadier,
some Milford Haven
or a Noël Coward;
the almond shampoo
yes ...
Do I mind a girl?
Her fingers, long, feel
like Medusa's snakes;
water does not splash
nor is it hot,
but bubbles warm
ah .....
Her name is
Alphonsina Sir
not Spanish,
Neapolitan.
This agony of fumigating bliss
and lime conditioner;
I scent the weedy pungent Med.
My parting's now on the wrong side
and then it's not,
but am I being modelled,
Snipped like a Sassoon?
Oh, it tastes,
this soft and muscly mistral breeze
has me succumbed to sturdiness
and corpulence around my angled chair
and dancing round are Borbons and bambini.
But now ...
I have to bid farewell to lovely Alphonsina
who waves a golden smile
under my umbrella
into the mist and fog.
Nothing is more English I was told
Than Trumper's in Curzon Street.

DRINKS

'You are so wonderful chérie!'
(Look left look right does she mean me?)
'I'm Fifi Kitson come to my party'
They were there
the beautiful people
the grand
the meek
the tall
the short
the wits
the arty
at her party
I met her cousin Charles Dupont
had I not been to old Vermont?
I reversed into the Minister's horse's neck and made an apology
and then succumbed to the usual tautology
I saw Don Giovanni well past his prime
the girl on his arm was at least thirty-nine.
'Good evening Count, hallo Monsignor,
I'm expected at home, no thank you no more'
'Darling where were you? You're going away
come meet Mohammed and Tanya and stay'
'Fifi I'm late, two hours at least'
'If you leave now I shall call you a beast!'
Kiss kiss pout pout
A wave and a shout
And then
I was out.

THE SAVANT

In a sumptuous stately ballroom where the candelabra glitter;
At select thé-dansants where 'la jeunesse' is seen to flitter;
At soirées where a dowager will have her little titter;

There one finds with poise and grace,
A charming smile upon his face,
A fine example of our race,

His name oft' feared so much we know,
's Antoine Marie Xuereb Rizzo.

About one's blood - he knows it all:
Great Grandmamma and cousin Paul?
'You need not fret, 'twas long ago
How the resemblance shows up oh!

All antique dealers of known repute,
All famous artists without dispute,
All able critics of wit astute:

Have all joined hands and are at par,
Have spread his fame to lands afar,
Have hailed a 'cyclopaedia.

He is esteemed by high and low
's Antoine Marie Xuereb Rizzo.

'There's Mrs Oh, oh! don't you know?
They've just sold her a fake bureau;
And Josephine Spiteri Gibbons
Has just acquired a Mrs Siddons.'

He sent a newsy letter from the Orient Express;
He'd wined and dined at Belvoir with the you-know-whos no le
And Glyndbourne was a bore this year and cause of much distre
'But the Castelletti desk is mine;
It's time you tried my Rothschild wine;
There's now A Gobelins where I dine.'

It's Lock's and Lobb's and Saville Row,
For Antoine Marie Xuereb Rizzo.

He is the kindliest of men,
And one has heard it said from Cowes
To Christie's, Lord's and Sadlers Wells,
From Birzebbugia to Bombay,
From Cortina to San Tropez,
From here and there
And everywhere.

He lives a life of muted grace,
At an aristocratic pace,
As in the days when men wore lace.

He is so pleased to talk about
A cornice, or what's in or out;
An heirloom worn upon the breast,
His eyes are sharp: this is the test!
And thus he speaks this man of taste,
'I think her baubles are all paste!
The mounting's old, they've sold the stones
To pay for Uncle Victor's loans;
How sad, a gift from Carolina
Queen of Naples to Teresina.'

Sotto voce - no one heard,
He would never spread the word,
The C.I.R. that man so grim
Would not ever hear from him,
Of course he'll help whene'er he can,
He is a kind and gentle man.

He is esteemed by high and low,
's Antoine Marie Xuereb Rizzo.

Their daddies paid ten thousand bucks
For what young ladies outght to know,
The boyfriends growled and said, 'Aw shucks.'
But mommas said, 'They gotta go.'

Thus waved the Hanks and Blakes and Earls
As Q.E. II slid out of port
And took the precious southern girls
To Britain that they might all get
The rudiments of etiquette.

Their teacher's name was Peggy Hallis,
She started off with Blenheim Palace.
'Did your girls like Singer Sargent?
All the pictures of Consuelo?'
'Carrie! Shelley! tell the Baron
What you liked in Blenheim Palace;
What you thought of our Consuelo.
'Hey Miss Hallis I dunno! So?'

The Earl of Bradford's for the night,
'He's a very charming guy,
The house is kinda old,
A Georgian castle,
But siree ...! I think he ought'r
Make more sure he's got hot water.'

'Now Lady Spencer she's just great,
A truly Royal lady.'
They drank Champagne in her front room
Then curtsied to the Earl's old groom
And called his lordship 'porter'.

'A lord took us around his zoo,
We met a knight of Malta too,
We wenna Harrods and some place
All wearin' hats for this horse race.
I tell yer, we have done it all,
Our trip to Britain was a ball,
Don't speak to us of etiquette,
We're the real snooty set!
Hi Hank, it.. was..just.. g r e a t,
Want some candy? Wanna date?

Adelina
liked Mdina
so did
Agatina
Carmelina
Teresina
and
Giuseppina
but
Marie
liked the sea
and the klima
of Sliema.

People called Gatto
play scacco matto
in their salotto

Others called Gatt
do that
in their club or mess
that is where they play chess.

Alice Borg is a Mifsud
Her husband Charlie Grech
Is a Bonello
Their daughter Marianne
Is pure Zammit
And little Eddie
Is a true Castillo.

Mr Sammut
Wore a new suit
Miss Pellegrini
A bikini
Petit
For tea
Dr Reynaud
Just would not go
Dr Randon
Had gone
Mr Tonna Barthet
Ordered café
He could not agree
With Dr Dupuis
Who was causing a stir
So Mr Gollcher
Had to complain
Again.

Marthese and Marvic
Were solid good friends
So this story starts
And happily ends
At home at Maron
Or at home at Majohny
With Marthese and her John
Marvic and her Ronnie.

Sir Arturo Mercieca
Looked out of the tieqa;
Sir Luigi Camilleri
Thought it quite dreary;
Sir Philip Pullicin
Said, 'Għandek il-ħin?'
Sir Luigi Preziosi
Said, 'Nobody passes
I can see all three of you need new glasses'

Ċens Depasquale read and read
And kept each tome inside his head
Recalling well, 'no need to try'
He saw it all in his mind's eye.

'Sir Hannibal you're looking fine.'
'You know I've just reached ninety-nine,
I'm going now to get some peace.'
'No! no! let's pray your years increase.'
'I'm only going off to Nice.'

The de Piros like spaghetti,
The Magris ravioli,
The Doublesins timpana,
The Coleiros canneloni.

They savoured an aperitif,
Thanked God for the good wine,
Each toasted one another,
And settled down to dine.

They liked the view, the calma,
They praised the cook as well,
They spoke of politicians,
And all started to yell.

The clergy was discussed at length,
And here they waxed quite lyric,
They laughed and laughed and laughed again,
About some panegyric.

The choice today was dentici,
Or trill or fried lampuka,
And fresh ġbejniet, souffle,
And coffee and Sambuca.

Whoever's turn, he paid the bill,
They kissed and left quite late,
And said ten times as they went out,
'Next Thursday then at eight.'

John Hookham Frere
Had gone quite spare
His gardener had orders
Concerning borders
They were to be bright and creditable
And not all vegetable.

Sir Bartle Frere
Sat in his chair
And while he spoke he shook 'em

He read a tome
Of Greece and Rome
By his old uncle Hookham.

Josef Anton Grech Manduca
Bought and flew a German stuka
Then he put it in his drawing room for all to looka
tit
mit
Evvy, Caruanell, Saverin and Grizu
And sometimes with Zizu.

The Pullicinos
were eleven bambinos
which is how they began
to become a clan

Professor Ganado
was an aficionado
of heated orations
concerning Freemasons

Mrs Xriha
bought her fwieħa
on the cheap
the creep

Madame Manfrè
la la la le
You've sewn me a bodice
Which makes me a goddess

The Parlatos
Dined with the Amatos
The Camilleris
Heard it next day
The news could have reached
The Cremonas
But they had all
Gone away.

The Carob tree is round and dark
And rough and rugged is its bark
Its pods grow ominous, grotesque
Nor is it even picturesque,
Oh dear it's rather ugly

It is redeemed in lovers eyes!
For it has caused so many ties,
For although it is ugly
It is secure and snugly.

The white and fluffy Maltese dog
So small and sweet to cuddle
It bounced about and yapped and yapped
And always caused a muddle;

Oh Mariannina died of shame
It was Gobelins, in the middle
Of Countess Sant's armorial pouf
Where Nufa did her piddle.

If I said things that were said by old Pike
I could send all the workers on strike
And the grand and the vain
Would perform in some pain
If we laughed at their antics like Pike.

If in fact I could, I would be
An egg-head of philosophy
The sort that shows dafter
Life's tears and laughter
Than they could possibly be.

The masses are mighteous
And always self-righteous
It's not easy to be
For individuality

The voice of the masses
Is always in tune
With what I believe in
This afternoon

The masses comprise
What it takes to be wise
But they cannot explain
Without going insane

The Opposition thunders
Unconsciously one wonders
Would the country benefit from powerful dominion?
Or should there be more than one opinion?

Dom's friends say he is a toff
And George was a big swell
They'll surely meet again some day
And have a chat in heaven

Oh dear oh dear oh dear oh Dom
Where oh where did it come from?
Did you make us free as air
Or was it George Borg Olivier?

Michelangelo Merisi da Caravaggio
Was famous not only for his chiaro scuro but also for his braggadochio and cora
I'm far better he claimed
Than Buonarotti and named
His assets in dreadful linguaggio.

Death dispossessed Louis Quatorze
When he was pulling up his drawers;
He later turned on Louis Quinze
While he was making other plans;
And then, so fast with all his cares
He took a chop at Louis Seize;
I am afraid I don't pretend
To know the other Louis' end;
But since the line of Louis started
It seems that all have now departed.

Sir Maurice and Lady Dorman - Oh what delight!
You dressed for breakfast, lunch and dinner every morning, noon and nigh
For ten years you lived with fallacies,
Obsequies, courtesies, in palaces,
And, if one might:
You looked quite a regal sight.

There once lived on Comino
A wizard called Nino
Whose potions were known to be strong
He created four blizzards
Two-tailed spotted lizards
And sometimes burst into song.

The C. of E's a bit slipshod
In laying down the laws of God
The Catholics, who are not so free,
Eschew their plights in casuistry

There was a sad lady of Qrendi
Rebuffed by a Turk called Effendi
It was with a smirk
That this wicked old Turk
When confronted just said, 'I pretendi.'

There was a poseur from Sannat
Who gilded the wheels of his cart
He festooned his old mule
And his goat in pink tulle
Then behaved like a man set apart.

There was a young flirt from Hal Far
Who dined with a girl from Zabbar
Whose father proclaimed
They be wed or defamed
'cos he heard they had gone far too far.

There was an old man of Zebbug
With an income uncommonly huge
He would spread it around
All the village and found
Consolation and welcome refuge.

There was a great sage from Zejtun
Who gazed all he could at the moon
He predicted he might
Tire of the same sight
And confessed that it should be quite soon.

A thinker once left Mġarr
And travelled the world in his car
He saw every sight
By day and by night
But preferred his village by far

There was an old count of Mdina
Whose great love was simply called Gina
She had no one to blame
For her lack of surname
In fact it made the Count keener.

There was a fishmonger of Malta
Whose love led him straight to the altar
She became such a shrew
He knew not what to do
In the end he decided to salt her.

There was a good fisherman who
Claimed little there was that he knew
Of matters of state
Or the taxation rate
And that fishing was all he could do.

There was once in old St Paul's Bay
A doctor who said he was gay
His sparce knowledge of jargon
Led him into a bargain
About which he'd rather not say.

There was an old farmer of Dingli
Who often complained he felt tingly
He was given some lotion
But no use was the potion
His trouble was just living singly.

There was a fine girl of Hamrun
Who promised her suitor that soon
She would love him and when
The thing happened that then
She would wed him that same afternoon.

There was a young blade of Birgu
Who never saw anything through
He considered three cousins
Two sisters and dozens
Of ladies whom he thought might do.

A truculent man called Cassar
Acquired his assets at par
He'd hold on a bit
And sometimes would sit
Till his profit was greater by far.

There was a young lady of Xlendi
Who converted her old name to Wendy
She swam in the buff
Displaying her fluff
And everyone thought she was trendy.

A dreamy Sliemite called Pace
Fell deeply for Juliette Stafrace
His love of the girl
Sent him into a whirl
That lasted from April till March.

The dark-eyed air hostess said, "I
Wish to make things just right when you fly."
I press-buttoned a call
And she kept me in thrall
So I think of Air Malta and sigh.

There was a young woman at peace,
Who found her best source of release
Was a shrill scream at dawn
Prone upon a mown lawn
Or a week with her lover in Greece.

Hand it to Paul Xuereb 'twas his
That idea for whiz indices
"Eureka," he shouted
Then happily sprouted
A bibliography of bibliographies.

CLERIHEWS

The women of Kalafrana
Eat lots of banana
They sit in the sun
And eat one.

The traders of Marsaxlokk
Never take stock
For years and years
They're in arrears.

A nice girl from Gudja
Sang do re mi fa
But she would not go
To sol la ti do.

The ladies of San Martin
Are always serene
Except in June
For the full moon.

A girl from Floriana
Became a sultana
Her sire had others
All very good mothers.

The night watchmen of Ħaġar Qim
It would seem
Slept soundly on the sacrificial altar
One night Joey and one night Walter.

The men of Żurrieq
Are always so quieq
They are the chagrin
Of the men of Tarxien.

A cobbler of Paola
Used words that were fowler
Than a Luqa man would
Or could.

Jenoveffa Bianchi
Fell for a junkie
It was in May
And it lasted a day.

Geoffrey Sultana
Some called 'the Pirana'
A very odd name
For someone so tame.

Peter Paul Cremona
Got a degree from Barcelona
He holds the record to date
With another forty-eight.

Paul Zammit
Joined the elite
He had an eye
For a good buy.

A Lija physician
Felt in a position
Where he could expect
A little respect.

A Rabat patrician
Was no politician
The more he was stirred
The less anyone cared.

Here lies Alfred always weary
Trusting none and ever dreary.

Here lies Mr Fenech who thought he knew
So much more than me and you.

Here lies John Francia to be mused upon
He deigned to wait around a bit and then moved on.

Here lies the old Archbishop whose buckles and lace
I remember better than his face.

Here lies Lisa a lifelong retailer
Who sold her wares to any sailor.

Here lies Annetta of Mdina
For most of her life no one had seen her.

Here lies George who brought freedom for all
He stood   five and a half feet tall.

Here lies Pike, all laughed at his wit
He spoke of life, but didn't believe in it.

Here lies the greatest fool it has been said
Beside him a professor, also dead.

INDEX OF FIRST LINES